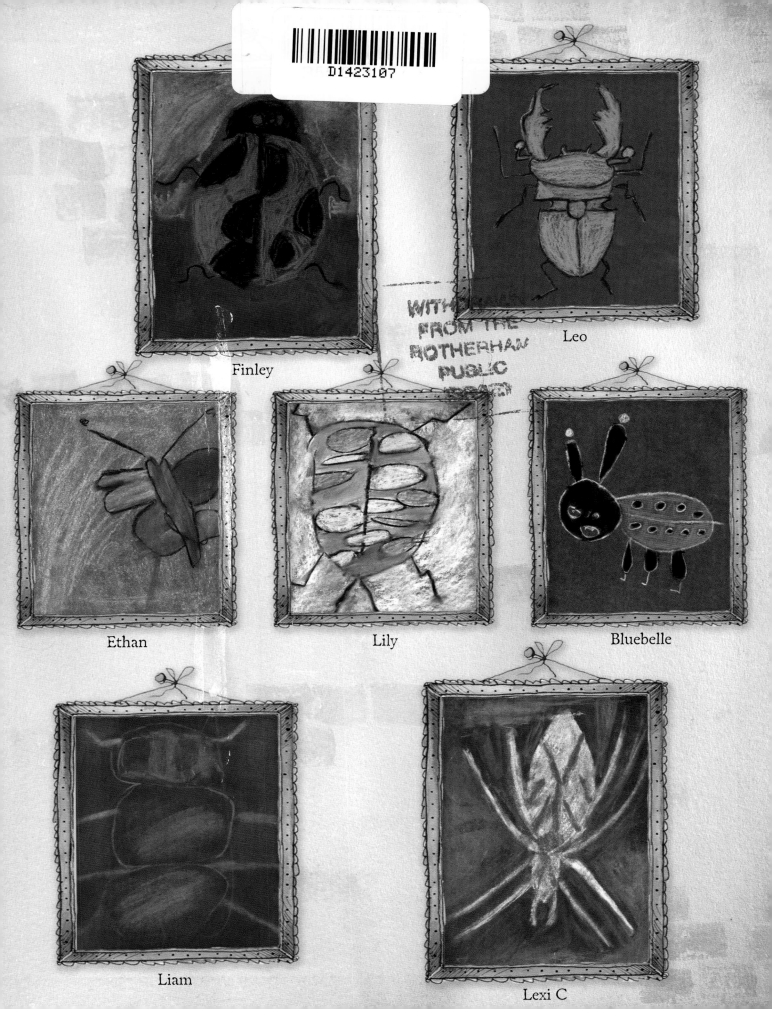

Finley

Leo

Ethan

Lily

Bluebelle

Liam

Lexi C

Thank you to Thameside Primary School, Abingdon for helping with the endpapers.

The publisher would like to thank Zoe Simmons, Oxford Museum of Natural History, for her help and enthusiasm.

For beautiful little Olive—V.T.

To Ola and Amelia, with love—K.P.

OXFORD
UNIVERSITY PRESS

Great Clarendon Street, Oxford OX2 6DP

Oxford University Press is a department of the University of Oxford. It furthers the University's objective of excellence in research, scholarship, and education by publishing worldwide. Oxford is a registered trade mark of Oxford University Press in the UK and n certain other countries

Text copyright © Valerie Thomas 2019
Illustrations copyright © Korky Paul 2019
The moral rights of the author and artist have been asserted

Database right Oxford University Press (maker)

First published in 2019

British Library Cataloguing in Publication Data available

ISBN: 978-0-19-276760-8 (hardback)

10 9 8 7 6 5 4 3 2 1

Printed in China

Paper used in the production of this book is a natural, recyclable product made from wood grown in sustainable forests. The manufacturing process conforms to the environmental regulations of the country of origin

www.winnieandwilbur.com

VALERIE THOMAS AND KORKY PAUL

Winnie and Wilbur
THE BUG SAFARI

OXFORD
UNIVERSITY PRESS

Winnie the Witch and her big black cat
Wilbur were having a picnic in the garden.
Winnie took a big bite out of her muffin
and crumbs dropped into the grass.

Ants rushed to collect them,
and Winnie bent down to watch.

'Look at those ants,
Wilbur,' Winnie said.
'The crumbs they
are carrying
are bigger
than they are.
Isn't that amazing?'

Winnie lay in the grass
to watch the ants.

A shiny red beetle pounced on a crumb and ate it.
Then a red and yellow caterpillar with green spikes
and purple spots came crawling along.

'Blithering broomsticks,' Winnie said.
'That's an incredible caterpillar, Wilbur.'
That *is* an incredible caterpillar,
thought Wilbur. I wonder what it tastes like?

'Wouldn't it be fun to be as small
as bugs, Wilbur?' said Winnie.
'Then we could *really* see what
they are doing.'

'**Meow**,' said Wilbur.
He didn't think that would be fun.

Then Winnie had a very good idea.
Well, she had an idea. She waved
her magic wand, shouted,

'Abracadabra!'

and Winnie and Wilbur were tiny.
Wilbur was really, really tiny.
'Meow,' said Wilbur.
Well, it was more like '<small>meow</small>'.

He was frightened.
The ants looked big.
The beetle looked huge.
The caterpillar looked enormous.
I hope it doesn't eat me, Wilbur thought.

The ants were busily carrying
the crumbs to their nest.
Some of them ran across Wilbur's tail.
'Meow,' cried Wilbur.
He didn't like ants running across his tail.

'Look out, Wilbur,' squeaked Winnie
in her tiny voice. 'Mind your tail!
There's a centipede coming!'
Too late.

'Meow, ow,' cried poor Wilbur.

The shiny red beetle was watching them.

Did beetles eat tiny witches and really, really tiny cats? No, luckily they liked muffin crumbs.

Tweet, tweet, tweet.
A bird landed in the grass.
It was looking for its lunch.

A nice fat worm?
Or a tiny witch and a really,
really tiny cat?

Luckily it found a nice fat worm.

Suddenly the ground began to shake.
Something enormous was coming.
Clomp! Clomp! Clomp!

What could it be?

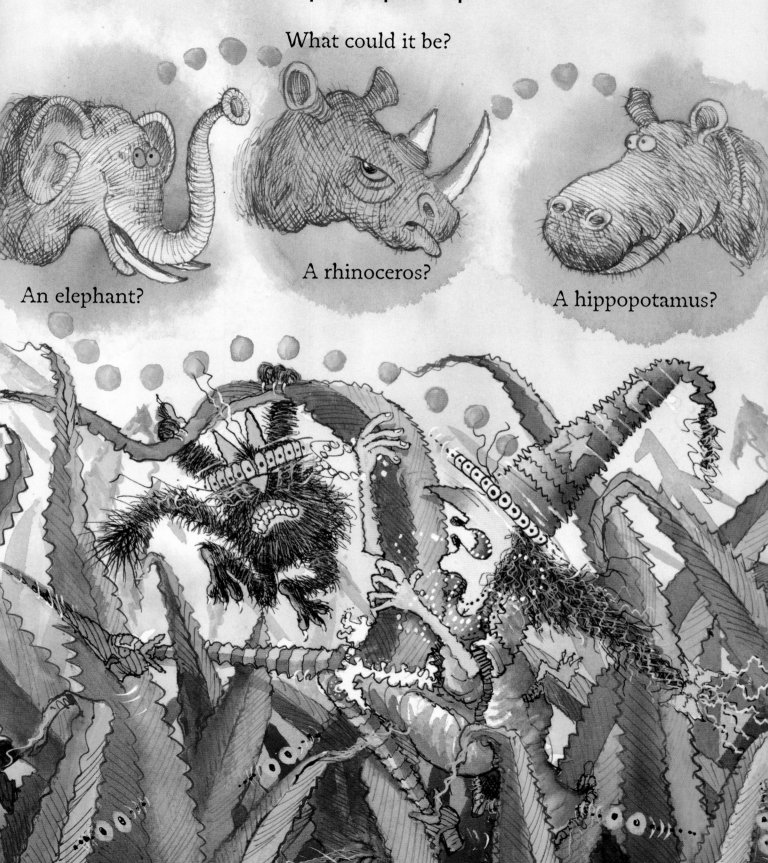

A rhinoceros?

An elephant?

A hippopotamus?

Two gigantic boots clomped across the grass.
It was the postman bringing Winnie's letters.

'Run! Run, Wilbur!' shrieked Winnie.
'If the postman stands on us
we'll be squashed.'

'I made a mistake,' Winnie said.
'I made us too small. I'll make
another spell to make us big again.
Where is my wand, Wilbur?'

But the wand wasn't in the grass.
It was stuck high up in a prickly rose bush.
And it was still the same size.

'Oh dear, oh dear,' cried Winnie. 'How
will we ever get up there, Wilbur?'

Just then the incredible caterpillar crawled past.

It started to climb up the rose bush. Winnie and Wilbur jumped onto the caterpillar's back and held onto its spikes.

Up, up up went, around the prickles, up to the wand.

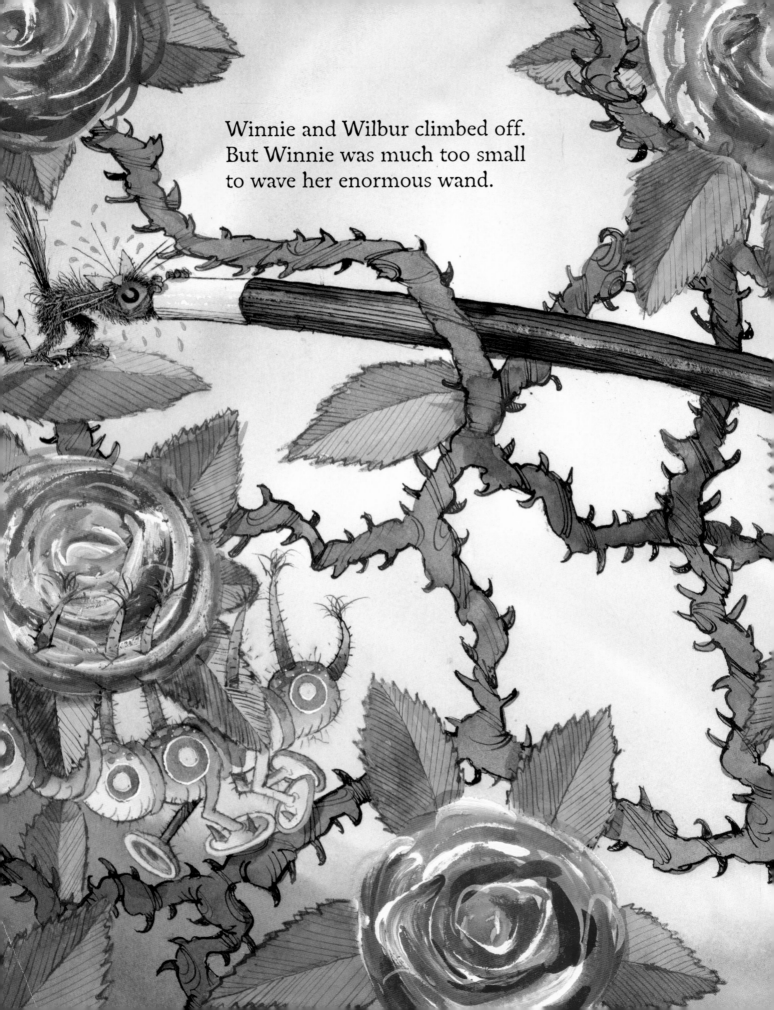

Winnie and Wilbur climbed off.
But Winnie was much too small
to wave her enormous wand.

Winnie pulled while Wilbur pushed,
but the wand didn't move at all.
'It's no good, Wilbur,' Winnie said.
'We'll have to stay this size for ever.'

'Meoooow,' cried Wilbur.

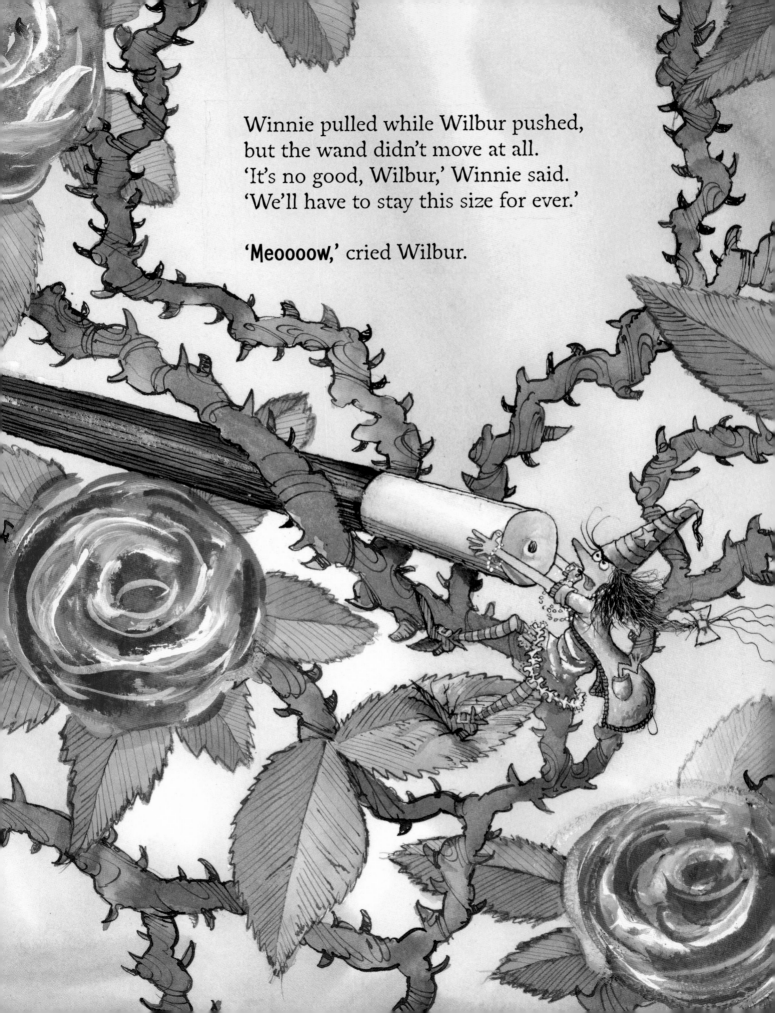

A hairy spider was spinning
a web among the roses.
She scuttled across, spun a long thread,
then twisted it around the wand.

Winnie, Wilbur, and the spider
pulled hard on the thread but
they couldn't move the wand.

A passing bumblebee flew on to the thread.
A big green grasshopper jumped up.
And a ladybird hung on.
Then the enormous caterpillar crawled over to help.

The wand began to wobble, the thread broke, and . . .

'Abracadabra!' squeaked Winnie as the wand waved in the air.

. . . . WHOOSH!

And Winnie and Wilbur
were back to their right size.
'I think we'll stay this size, Wilbur,'
Winnie said. 'It's a good size to be.'

'Purr, purr, purr,' said Wilbur.

Phoebe

Sebastian

Lexi B

Poppy C-J

Samgyang

Zuzanna

Theo